Jeanie & Genie

BROTHER BE GONE!

BY **TRISH GRANTED**
ILLUSTRATED BY **MANUELA LÓPEZ**

LITTLE SIMON
New York London Toronto Sydney New Delhi

LITTLE SIMON

An imprint of Simon & Schuster Children's Publishing Division · 1230 Avenue of the Americas, New York, New York 10020 · First Little Simon paperback edition September 2021 • Copyright © 2021 by Simon & Schuster, Inc. All rights reserved, including the right of reproduction in whole or in part in any form. LITTLE SIMON is a registered trademark of Simon & Schuster, Inc., and associated colophon is a trademark of Simon & Schuster, Inc. For information about special discounts for bulk purchases, please contact Simon & Schuster Special Sales at 1-866-506-1949 or business@simonandschuster.com. The Simon & Schuster Speakers Bureau can bring authors to your live event. For more information or to book an event contact the Simon & Schuster Speakers Bureau at 1-866-248-3049 or visit our website at www.simonspeakers.com. Designed by Brittany Fetcho • Manufactured in the United States of America 0721 MTN 10 9 8 7 6 5 4 3 2 1 • Library of Congress Cataloging-in-Publication Data • Names: Granted, Trish, author. | López, Manuela, 1985- illustrator. | Granted, Trish. Jeanie & genie ; 5. Title: Brother be gone! / by Trish Granted ; illustrated by Manuela Lopez. Description: First Little Simon paperback edition. | New York : Little Simon, an imprint of Simon & Schuster Children's Publishing Division 2021. | Series: Jeanie & genie ; 5 | Audience: Ages 5-9. | Audience: Grades K-1. | Summary: Jeanie's little brother Jake keeps annoying Jeanie, until finally she wishes him to disappear; unfortunately her friend Willow the genie (whose wish-granting powers are not exactly well controlled) is with her at the time—and now the girls have to figure out where Jake has gone and how to get him back. Identifiers: LCCN 2021007479 (print) | LCCN 2021007480 (ebook) | ISBN 9781534486997 (paperback) | ISBN 9781534487000 (hardcover) | ISBN 9781534487017 (ebook) Subjects: LCSH: Jinn—Juvenile fiction. | Wishes—Juvenile fiction. | Magic—Juvenile fiction. | Brothers and sisters—Juvenile fiction. | Best friends—Juvenile fiction. | CYAC: Genies—Fiction. | Wishes—Fiction. | Magic—Fiction. | Brothers and sisters—Fiction. | Best friends—Fiction. | Friendship—Fiction. Classification: LCC PZ7.1.G728 Br 2021 (print) | LCC PZ7.1.G728 (ebook) | DDC 813.6 [Fic]—dc23 LC record available at https://lccn.loc.gov/2021007479 LC ebook record available at https://lccn.loc.gov/2021007480

TABLE OF CONTENTS

Chapter 1

BROTHER, BROTHER GO AWAY

PLOP! Raindrops splashed against Willow Davis's bedroom window. She watched as they whizzed down the glass pane like little race cars zooming toward the finish line.

Willow knew she should be doing her chores or homework instead of daydreaming. Her room looked like a rainbow tornado had hit it, with brightly colored tights and sequined skirts in piles all over the floor.

I bet Jeanie's already checked off everything on her to-do list even though it's only Saturday, Willow thought with a smile.

Her best friend, Jeanie Bell, didn't daydream about race cars— she *was* one, zipping through school work and chores! But then, Jeanie had a lot of practice tackling homework. She'd always gone to Rivertown Elementary. Before Willow moved to Rivertown, she'd never done a lot of things *most* kids considered normal.

She'd never gone to a real school
with classes like math and science.
But she was an expert in astrology
and fairy tales!

She'd never tried butter pecan or
mint chocolate chip ice cream. But
she *had* tried a flavor that changed
color with your mood!

She'd never been camping or gone on class field trips. Once, she'd accidentally made an amusement park appear in her backyard, but that wasn't the same.

6

And she'd definitely never had a best friend before. Luckily, Jeanie was the best of the best. In fact, she was the only person outside of Willow's family who knew her big secret. The big secret that . . .

Willow Davis . . .

was actually . . .

a genie!

Another raindrop splattered against the window, jolting Willow back to reality. If she wanted to go over to Jeanie's house the next day, she had to finish all her work. It was time to make like a race car and step on the gas!

★★★

It was still raining on Sunday morning. Willow and Jeanie were hanging out in the Bells' den.

"What should we do?" asked Willow.

"Rain baseball!" shouted Jeanie's little brother Jake. "It's a new sport I invented. The bases are mud puddles!"

"Too wet. Too dirty. Too made-up," Jeanie told Jake. "Rainy days are for indoor games."

Jake stuck out his tongue.

Willow was feeling crafty, but Jeanie wanted to play a game of chess. So they compromised: Jeanie got out tubs of clay so they could sculpt their own chess pieces.

"Don't you just love mushing this stuff between your fingers?" Willow asked dreamily as she molded a small horse out of purple clay.

"I do! I do!" Jake shouted. "Gimme some!"

"Jake!" warned Jeanie. "This is *our* art project. Go find your own!"

As Jake scampered away, Willow watched Jeanie line up five little green pawns on the craft table and start on number six.

Seconds later, Jake was back with a sketchbook and some crayons. He slowly circled the girls, staring at them closely, then scribbling in his book.

Stare.

Scribble.

Stare.

Scribble.

Jeanie sighed. "What are you doing now?"

"Drawing you," said Jake, holding up his picture. "It's *my* art project."

Willow could tell Jeanie was annoyed. But personally she didn't mind Jake. She thought he was kind of funny. "He's just doing what you told him to," she pointed out to Jeanie.

"Yeah," said Jake. "I was just doing what you told me to." He smiled smugly.

Jeanie's eyes narrowed. "You're such a little monster!"

Jake's face lit up. "I *am* a monster," he agreed. Then he poked his fingers into Jeanie's green pawns and held up his hand. "The Booger Monster!"

He skipped around the girls,  waving his hand and singing *"Booger Monster! Booger Monster!"* at the top of his lungs.

Willow couldn't help but laugh a little bit. But Jeanie was *not* amused.

Chapter 2

SISTER AMBUSH SURPRISE!

"Moooooom!" Jeanie yelled. "Jake ruined my chess pieces!"

Mrs. Bell appeared in the doorway, hands on her hips.

"Is that true?" she asked Jake.

He nodded sheepishly.

"I think it's time for you to leave the girls alone," she told him.

Jake wiggled his eyebrows. "You haven't seen the last of the Booger

17

Monster!" he said, and scurried out of the den.

"Let's go to my room," Jeanie suggested. "Where we won't be disturbed."

"You have to admit Jake's got some artistic flair," said Willow as they went upstairs. "He really captured your scowl."

"Gee, thanks." Jeanie was just about to open her door when—

"ROOOOOOOOAAAAAAAR!" Jake leaped out of the linen closet at them.

Jeanie and Willow practically jumped out of their skin.

"Sister Ambush Surprise!" yelled Jake.

"You . . . you . . . ugh!" Jeanie cried. "I wish you would GO AWAY!"

But when she realized what she'd just said, Jeanie's stomach dropped. She'd made a wish. And with a friend like Willow around, wishes could be downright dangerous!

If someone made a wish while looking directly into Willow's eyes, Willow *had* to grant it. On top of that, Willow was a genie-in-*training*, and she was still learning to control her wish granting.

Then Jeanie realized something. *I wasn't looking at Willow. I was looking at Jake.* She breathed a sigh of relief. *That was close!*

"The Booger Monster strikes again!" laughed Jake.

Jeanie rolled her eyes. "Just leave me alone, okay?"

"Fine, Meanie Jeanie!" Jake stuck his tongue out at her again and ran to his bedroom.

"Jake's not so bad," Willow offered as she followed Jeanie down the hall. "He just wants to hang out with his big sister."

Jeanie collapsed onto her perfectly made bed. She knew Willow was right.

But then she glanced at the photo she'd tacked to her bulletin board. It was from the Bells' last beach vacation. The sun was shining, the waves were calm, and her parents looked totally relaxed. But all Jeanie saw was Jake crossing his eyes, giving her bunny ears, and ruining a perfectly nice family portrait.

"I love Jake. Of course, I do," she told Willow, staring deep into her friend's green eyes. "But look at that picture. Everything's always a joke to him. Sometimes I wish he'd just disappear!" She flopped back down on the bed.

Suddenly a burst of golden light
filled the room.

Chapter 3

THE DISAPPEARANCE OF JAKE

Willow reached for the lamp charm she always wore around her neck. It was warm. An electric feeling prickled at the back of her neck. She knew what that meant. . . .

Willow picked up Jeanie's stuffed tiger, Mr. Whiskers, and stroked his silky fur. "Um, Jeanie . . . ," she began nervously.

"What?" Jeanie's voice was

muffled by the stacks of pillows she'd face-planted into.

"You just made a wish."

Jeanie didn't look up. "No I didn't."

Willow tossed Mr. Whiskers at Jeanie. "Yes … you did," she insisted. "You said you love Jake, but that sometimes you wish he'd disappear."

Jeanie sat up. "I didn't say that. I couldn't have. If I said that . . ."

Then Willow watched as the realization set in. Jeanie started to breathe faster. Her hands went to her mouth. Her eyes went wide.

Willow followed Jeanie's gaze to the bulletin board. Something was suddenly different about that vacation photo they'd been looking at. But what was it?

Willow gasped. Jake! He was now missing from the photo!

"No. This *cannot* be happening!" cried Jeanie.

Willow could tell how panicked her friend was. And she was pretty freaked out too. But she knew she needed to try to keep Jeanie calm. "We don't know if anything's wrong yet," she said in as gentle a voice as possible. "Let's just go find Jake. Once we find him, we won't have to worry!"

The girls raced down the hallway toward Jake's room. Or toward what *used* to be Jake's room. The door to the bedroom was . . . gone. The whole room had completely vanished.

This is bad, thought Willow. *Really bad.*

Jake wasn't eating a snack in the kitchen. Or playing in the backyard. Or coloring in the den. His toys were missing, his crayons nowhere to be found. Even the dents Jake had made in Jeanie's chess pieces were gone.

This could only mean one thing. Willow had made Jeanie's wish come true.

And now Jake had disappeared!

Chapter 4

TABLE FOR THREE?

"What are we going to do?" Jeanie asked as she paced back and forth. "My parents are going to flip out!"

"Um . . . maybe we shouldn't mention it just yet," said Willow nervously. "At least, not until we figure out how to get Jake back."

Jeanie stopped pacing. Willow was right. They needed to have a plan before they said *anything* to

39

her parents. Plus, explaining things would mean revealing Willow's secret. That was against the World Genie Association's rules and could mean big trouble for Willow.

"For now, let's just tell them Jake's cleaning the attic," Willow suggested. "Or giving Bear a dog bath. Or bringing some cookies to Mr. Penny next door."

Jeanie appreciated Willow's suggestions, but her parents wouldn't believe *any* of those.

DING-DONG!

"Girls," called Jeanie's dad. "Willow's mother is here to pick her up!"

Jeanie and Willow glanced nervously at each other. Jeanie knew they couldn't hide up here forever.

They were going to have to face her parents—and whatever questions they might ask.

Jeanie got more and more nervous with each step she took down the stairs.

But when they got to the front door, they found Jeanie's parents chatting happily with Mrs. Davis.

"We love having Willow over," Jeanie's mom was saying. "She's such a ray of sunshine!"

Mrs. Davis smiled. "We feel the same way about Jeanie. You really have such a lovely family."

Please don't mention Jake. Please don't mention Jake, thought Jeanie. And to her amazement . . . no one said a word.

As Willow and her mom said their goodbyes, Willow shot Jeanie one last apologetic look. And then Jeanie was on her own.

"Who's hungry?" said Jeanie's dad. "The roast chicken is almost ready for our Sunday family dinner."

"Jeanie, could you set the table?" her mom asked.

While her parents got things ready in the kitchen, Jeanie grabbed the plates and silverware. In a daze, she headed to the dining room. It would normally have been Jake's night to set the table, but her mom hadn't even noticed.

Once Jeanie was done setting the table, she sat down and waited for her parents to bring in the food. Finally, they entered with the chicken and a bowl of mashed potatoes. Jeanie was sure they were going to realize that something was very wrong. But they only had one question.

"Who's this fourth table setting for?" Jeanie's dad asked her. "Are you expecting company?"

Jeanie's mouth dropped open. It was like Jake didn't exist! She desperately wanted to say to her parents, *It's for Jake! Remember, your son?* But she had promised Willow she wouldn't say anything yet. And she really didn't want to spoil Willow's secret. So she tried to cover herself.

"It's . . . um . . . it's for Bear," she stammered. "He's family, right?"

"He certainly is." Her dad laughed. "And there's nothing more important than family. But I don't think the dog belongs at the table."

Bear must have heard his name—
and he must have been hungry—
because he trotted into the dining
room and snatched a shred of
chicken off Jeanie's plate.

"Bear!" shouted Jeanie's dad.
But he was laughing, and so was her
mom.

Jeanie twisted her napkin nervously. No Jake. No questions. No trouble. That was a good thing, right?

Right?

Chapter 5

GLASS HALF FULL

On Monday morning, Willow woke with a knot in the pit of her stomach. She had never made a person disappear before. Unless you counted the time she'd *thought* she'd made the Berriman twins vanish. But that had turned out to be a misunderstanding. This time she'd done a vanishing act for real!

Luckily, Willow was a glass-half-full

53

kind of girl. She couldn't help looking on the bright side of any situation. Since Jeanie hadn't meant her wish *literally*, maybe the magic would wear off more quickly?

I bet Jake's already turned up, she told herself. By the time she'd gotten dressed in her lucky ladybug tights and put on her jingly bracelets, she was sure of it.

But when Willow arrived in classroom 2B and saw the look on Jeanie's face, she didn't feel quite so sunny anymore.

Willow glanced around. No one could hear them except the class hamster, Jelly Bean.

"How's Jake?" she asked Jeanie tentatively.

Jeanie shook her head. "I wouldn't know. He's still missing!"

Willow's heart sank. That was what she'd been hoping *not* to hear.

"Willow, we *have* to fix this!" Jeanie said.

"I know we do," said Willow. "I'm just not exactly sure how."

Willow tried to remember what her genie manual said about vanishing, but she hadn't exactly gotten to that chapter yet.

"Once, I made a toad vanish with a wart-be-gone spell," she explained. "That doesn't work on people for obvious reasons. Plus, I never made it reappear. It had gotten into the house, and I didn't exactly *want* it to come back. Though now that I think about it, I do still hear a strange croaking sound in the bathroom sometimes, and—"

"Earth to Willow!" Jeanie interrupted. "I don't need a toad. I need a Jake."

"There's only one thing to do," said Willow. "Research. My mom's library is sure to have the solution. Come over after school and we can start looking for it."

For the first time all morning, Jeanie smiled. "Fixing a problem with research? I think I can do that!"

Chapter 6

HOME IS WHERE THE MAGIC HAPPENS

Later that afternoon, Jeanie followed Willow up the path to the Davises' house. She was so glad her parents had said she could go there after school. Partly because she and Willow needed to figure out how to get Jake back.

But also partly because Jeanie had never been to Willow's house before! Would there be floating beds and talking mirrors? Faucets dripping with rainbows or ceilings that glittered with stars? She couldn't wait to see a real genie house!

But as Willow gave her the grand tour through the kitchen, den, and dining room, everything was surprisingly . . . normal. Even Willow's room, with its canopy bed and colorful mess, was pretty standard.

"I guess I was expecting it to be more magical," Jeanie admitted.

"Nope," said Willow. "Just a typical house on a typical block. There's only one room that's not so typical: my mom's office."

She led Jeanie to a room at the end of the hallway. Willow's mom was the president of the World Genie Association, and her work space was everything Jeanie had imagined and more.

The air smelled of scented candles and tea leaves, and the walls were covered in star charts and framed degrees in conjuring, enchantments, and astrology. A huge telescope pointed out the window, and a crystal ball sat on a stand next to the desk.

There was also a big bookshelf crammed with books with titles like *When You Wish upon a Star, Ladybugs and Other Lucky Omens,* and *Advanced Wishing for Advanced Genies.* That last book had a note taped on the front that read:

Advanced Wishing
for Advanced Genies

I mean it, Willow. These spells are for master genies ONLY. Don't even think about trying them!
—Mom

"Now this is more like it," said Jeanie. Then she turned to her best friend. "Remind me, why can't we just ask your mom for help?" That seemed like the practical thing to do.

Willow sighed. "Because if I ask for help, I won't get my next genie badge," she said. "And if I don't earn a badge in every magical skill—including vanishing—I'll never become a master genie."

Oh yeah, thought Jeanie. She knew that if she asked Willow to, her friend would skip trying for the badge so they could get Jake back. But becoming a master genie was Willow's dream, and the badges were important.

"All right," Jeanie said finally. "Let's do some research!"

The girls grabbed all the books they could carry and brought them into the den. For the next hour, Jeanie speed-read through *Magic Mayhem*, *Charms 101*, and *Sister Spells*. She read about memory enchantments and love potions and hypnotism. But she couldn't find anything that dealt with disappearing family members.

Just when she was starting to give up hope that she'd ever see Jake again—

"I've got it!" Willow shouted. "I think I know how to get your brother back."

REVERSE THE CURSE

Willow scooted closer to Jeanie and held up the book she'd been reading: *Accidental Magic in Everyday Homes.*

"There's a chapter called 'The Big Time Out: How to Make a Pesky Sibling Disappear,'" she explained.

Jeanie's eyes narrowed. "I think we've already mastered that."

Willow shook her head. "No,

look! Down at the bottom, there are instructions to *reverse* the curse."

THE TIME-OUT REVERSAL SPELL

So you've finally gotten rid of your pesky little brother. Congratulations!

But no time-out can last forever. To make your sibling reappear before your parents start asking questions, follow the instructions below. It's as easy as 1, 2, 3!

"How'd you know the spell could be undone?" asked Jeanie.

"Intuition," replied Willow.

The girls read over the instructions, step by step. Then they read them again. Willow didn't want to make any mistakes. They *had* to get Jake back.

"Ready to give the time-out reversal a try?" she asked.

"Let's do it!" Jeanie said. "For step one, we just need a pen and a piece of paper."

"On it!" Willow said. She grabbed a purple glitter pen and a notebook from a drawer, and handed them to Jeanie. "You can do this," Willow told her friend. "You're the best list maker I know!"

"Thanks," said Jeanie. Then she tapped the pen against her chin. "But this isn't a typical list."

"I'm going to give you some space," said Willow. "You'll have an easier time feeling inspired if I'm not staring at you." Her bracelets jingled as she hopped off the couch.

As she left the room, she heard the sound of the pen scratching across the page.

Willow had a good feeling about this plan. And her intuition was never wrong.

Well, almost never . . .

Chapter 8

IF THE HAT FITS . . .

Twenty minutes later, Jeanie set down the pen and stretched her arms. She felt okay about this.

Step one of the wish reversal was to make a list of things she truly loved about her brother.

1) Make a list of things
   I truly love about Jake ☺

✓ Jake is funny.
(Even though he jokes
around when he shouldn't,
sometimes he really makes people laugh.)

✓ Jake has a great imagination.
(The Booger Monster may be gross,
but it's pretty creative.)

✓ Jake is kind.
(He takes really good
care of Bear.)

✓ Jake really likes
hanging out with me.
(And I should be nicer to him.)

In the end, the list had been easier to write than Jeanie expected. She'd just needed to think about the problem logically. Even though Jake could be really annoying sometimes, he was a good brother.

Plus, he always lets me take the marshmallows from his cereal, she thought.

Jeanie tore her list out of the notebook. Then she went to look for Willow. She found her back in her mom's office, casually spinning a fancy-looking globe.

"Um, Willow, are you sure all that spinning isn't creating a tornado somewhere?" Jeanie joked.

Willow giggled. But she also stopped the globe mid-spin . . . just in case.

"My list is done!" Jeanie announced. "Now we have to find a hat." That was step two of the wish-reversal instructions.

"Do you think the *type* of hat matters?" Willow asked as she led Jeanie to her bedroom. "I've got an artsy beret, a flowered swim cap, and a pink plaid cowboy hat."

Jeanie opened Willow's closet.
"Is there anything more . . . Jake . . .
in here?"

Willow thought for a moment. Then her eyes lit up, and she reached to pluck something from the top shelf.

"How about this one?" she asked, holding up a WGA baseball cap. "I wore it when we played the WWA in last year's softball tournament."

"The WWA?" Jeanie asked.

"The World Wizard Association, of course," Willow replied. "They throw *wicked* curve balls."

Jeanie wanted to hear all about
the WWA, but they had more
important things to deal with at the
moment. "That one's perfect," she
said. "I mean, perfect for Jake. I
may not be very athletic, but I'll do
anything to get Jake back!"

"Even play rain baseball?" Willow asked.

"Even that." Jeanie shuddered. "And you know if I'm willing to play sports in the mud, I must be serious."

She just hoped it was enough to make the reverse curse work!

Chapter 9

SWEET AND SOUR

"Step three should be easy," said Willow as they headed to the kitchen. "We just need Jake's favorite food."

Jeanie made a face.

"Uh-oh. What is Jake's favorite food?" asked Willow.

"Sauerkraut," Jeanie replied.

"Really?!" Willow couldn't imagine any kid eating cabbage on purpose. Let alone *fermented* cabbage!

"Really," Jeanie said miserably.

Willow checked the refrigerator. "We've got sour pickles and sweet and sour shrimp, but no sauerkraut," she told Jeanie. "You're just going to have to wish for some."

Willow looked at Jeanie and waited. Nothing happened.

"Uh, Jeanie? For this to work, you actually have to make a wish," Willow reminded her. "And you have to mean it."

Willow knew that Jeanie got annoyed by Jake sometimes, but she also knew Jeanie genuinely did not mean to make him disappear.

Jeanie looked directly into Willow's eyes. "I wish I had some sauerkraut," she said.

An electric feeling prickled the back of Willow's neck as her lamp charm lit up with a golden glow.

And just like that, a jar of sauerkraut appeared on the kitchen counter!

"I don't know if I'll ever get used to that," said Jeanie with a laugh.

"Okay, last step," said Willow. "Why don't you go sit at the kitchen table while I get everything ready."

Willow folded Jeanie's list into a little butterfly and placed it inside the hat. Then she put the hat on Jeanie's head.

She grabbed a spoon, opened the jar, scooped up a big bite of sauerkraut, and held it out to Jeanie.

Jeanie's lips stayed clamped shut.

"It's only one bite," Willow whispered. "Do it for Jake."

Jeanie nodded. She took a deep breath, held her nose, and opened wide.

Down went the sauerkraut.

Down went the sibling feud.

Down went the girls' last hope of getting Jake back.

Then suddenly a brilliant flash of light lit up the kitchen. But before Willow had a chance to see if the spell had worked—

DING-DONG!

BROTHER COME BACK!

"That's my mom," said Jeanie nervously. "But your charm flashed! That means your magic did . . . something. Right?"

Willow nodded. "It must have. I just hope it was something good."

"I'll call you tonight and let you know if Jake is home," Jeanie said as she gathered her backpack and headed for the front door.

"Actually, you can't," Willow said, trailing after her. "We don't have a phone, remember? We only communicate by sending intentions out into the universe. It's not exactly reliable, though."

Jeanie had to laugh. She had forgotten this. Not having a phone wasn't very practical, but it was very . . . Willow. "Tomorrow at school then," Jeanie promised.

Willow opened the door for Mrs. Bell, who flashed the girls a big smile.

"Ready to go, sweetie?" she asked Jeanie.

Jeanie nodded as she and Willow followed Mrs. Bell outside.

Then something in the back seat of her mom's car caught Jeanie's eye. Something bouncy and giggly and little-brother shaped.

Jeanie's jaw dropped. "Is that Jake?" She couldn't believe her eyes. Had the wish reversal really worked?

"Yes. He wanted to come pick you up," Jeanie's mom answered. "I know you two don't always get along, but he really looks up to you."

Jeanie's cheeks flushed. She felt bad it had taken Jake disappearing for her to realize this, but she did love the kid.

When she turned back to Willow to say goodbye, she could see from the sparkle in her friend's eyes that Willow was just as happy as she was.

Suddenly the sound of wind chimes filled the air. A small sparkling cloud appeared, and a tiny golden box floated down toward Willow.

Jeanie's eyes got wide. She'd seen this happen before. It was how the WGA delivered badges! She stepped in front of Willow so that Willow could quickly grab the box without Jeanie's mom noticing.

"Tell me all about it tomorrow?" Jeanie whispered.

Willow nodded.

Jeanie wanted to hear every last detail about the badge. But right now there was something important she had to do: give her brother the biggest hug ever!

She waved goodbye to Willow and raced toward the car.